D0536509

This book is dedicated to
Jerry, Scott, mow Dog, Connie,
Carol, mark, and Grant
Love, Todd

This edition published by arrangement with Little, Brown
and Company (Inc.), New York, New York, USA. All rights reserved.

First published in Great Britain 2001
by Walker Books Ltd
87 Vauxhall Walk, London SE11 5HJ

This edition produced 2003 for
The Book People Ltd, Hall Wood Avenue,
Haydock, St Helens WA11 9UL

2 4 6 8 10 9 7 5 3 1

© 1999 Todd Parr

Printed in China

British Library Cataloguing in Publication Data:
a catalogue record for this book
is available from the British Library

ISBN 0-7445-8197-4

www.walkerbooks.co.uk

This Is My Hair

Todd Parr

TED SMART

This is my Hair
when I wake up

This is my Hair when I see a bear

This is my Hair
with a FLOWER in it

This is my Hair
at a rock Concert

This is my Hair
in pigtails

This is my Hair
when my Pigtails
are too tight

Ouch

This is my Hair with a bee in it

This is my Hair
after my brother Cut it

This is my Hair with
Spaghetti and meatballs
in it

This is my Hair with
soap in it

This is my Hair
when I'm painting

This is my Hair
when a Flying Saucer
Landed in it

This is my Hair in
the wind

This is my Hair in the snow

This is my Hair in Curlers

This is my Hair
with too much
hair Spray in it

This is my Hair
with my hat on

This is my Hair
with my hat OFF

This is my Hair
For School pictures

This is my Hair
with Gum in it

This is my Hair when I'm hanging upside down

This is me with
NO Hair

No matter
How your
Hair Looks,
Always Feel
Good about
Yourself.

Love,
Todd